Asiatic Black or Moon Bear
Lesser 'Red' Panda
Kinkajou
Ring-Tailed Cat
Giant Panda
Common Raccoons
Olingos
Coati

D1458544

Where bears, pandas and raccoons are found

to teachers and parents

This is a LADYBIRD LEADER book, one of a series specially produced to meet the very real need for carefully planned *first information books* that instantly attract enquiring minds and stimulate reluctant readers.

The subject matter and vocabulary have been selected with expert assistance, and the brief and simple text is printed in large, clear type.

Children's questions are anticipated and facts presented in a logical sequence. Where possible, the books show what happened in the past and what is relevant today.

Special artwork has been commissioned to set a standard rarely seen in books for this reading age and at this price.

Full colour illustrations are on all 48 pages to give maximum impact and provide the extra enrichment that is the aim of all Ladybird Leaders.

Acknowledgment

The world distribution map on the front endpaper is by Gerald Witcomb.

A Ladybird Leader

bears
and pandas

written and illustrated by John Leigh-Pemberton

Ladybird Books Loughborough

Bears

There are seven kinds *(species)* of bears.

They are in many ways rather like very large dogs, but they have short tails and eat any kind of food.

Brown Bear
2 m long and
up to 250 kg

Bears are dangerous animals.

Unlike cats or dogs,
they give no warning
before they attack.

In spite of their size
they can move very fast.

Bears: their senses

Bears have rather poor eyesight.
They make up for this
by having a wonderful sense
of smell.

All bears, except Polar Bears,
are active at night.

*American Black Bears
1.8 m long and up to
150 kg. They are
less dangerous
than Brown Bears
and are better climbers*

Bears: how they move

Bears walk with the sole of the foot
flat on the ground.

The word for this is *plantigrade.*

They are very good climbers
and can walk and balance
on their hind legs.

Brown Bears

Brown Bears were
once quite common in Europe,
North America and parts of Asia.

Because they sometimes killed cattle
they have been persecuted,
and many have been
destroyed.

European Brown Bear
Until about 900 AD
it was found in the
British Isles.
All bears can
'beg' naturally

*Syrian Brown Bear
It is paler and
smaller than the
European Bear*

*Baby bears are
the size of rats
when born*

Now there are
very few places in Europe
where bears remain.

In North America they survive
in Canada and Alaska
and in United States National Parks.

More about Brown Bears

Some Brown Bears eat
only vegetable food.

Others eat flesh as well.

The word for animals
which eat different kinds of foods
is *omnivorous.*

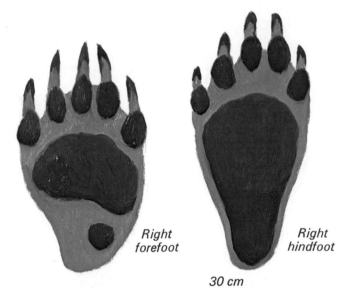

*Right
forefoot*

*Right
hindfoot*

30 cm

*The track of a Brown Bear (Europe).
Notice the five toes on each foot
and the long claws. These are the
bear's chief weapons*

There are Brown Bears living
in deserts and mountains.

These, like the Syrian Bear
and the Isabelline Bear,
are much paler in colour.

*The Isabelline Bear
from the Himalayas.
Like all Brown
Bears it lives
alone*

Grizzly Bears

Huge Brown Bears
living in North America
are called Grizzlies.

Once they were thought to belong
to a separate species.

Now they are quite rare.

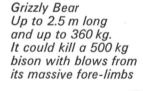

Grizzly Bear
Up to 2.5 m long
and up to 360 kg.
It could kill a 500 kg
bison with blows from
its massive fore-limbs

Grizzlies used to prey
upon the herds of bison.

When the bison became scarce
the Grizzlies became fewer too.

In some places the forests
where they lived
have been cut down.

Alaska (or Kodiak) Brown Bears

These are the largest
of all flesh-eating *(carnivorous)*
animals on land.

*Bears often wake in
milder spells of weather,
but their body
temperature does not
go down as in
true hibernation*

Like most bears,
Alaska Bears sleep
for much of the winter.

They do this in a den
in which their two cubs are born.

This winter sleep
is not true *hibernation*.

Alaska Brown Bear
3 m long and weighing 780 kg

American Black Bears

These bears can be
almost any colour.

Most are black, but there are
chocolate, tan, cinnamon, grey
and even white ones too.

They are very good climbers
and swim well.

Up to 1.8 m long and up to 150 kg

*American
Black Bear
Found from
N. Mexico,
through the
United States
to parts
of Canada*

Black Bears will eat
almost any kind of food.

They have learned to approach cars,
expecting to be fed.

But they are dangerous animals,
so it has been made illegal
to feed them.

*Anyone who really cares about
animals should remember not to
feed them from a car.
Because they become unafraid
of cars, some
animals will
stray onto
roads, where
they wait to
be fed.
In this way
many wild
animals have
been killed
or injured.*
So, don't feed!

The Spectacled Bear
or Andean Bear

This is the only bear
found south of the Equator.

It lives in forests
of the Andes mountains
in South America.

This small, intelligent bear
is quite rare.

Spectacled Bear
About 1.6 m long
and 140 kg in weight

These bears
live almost entirely
on leaves, fruit
and nuts.

They are believed
to make
nests of sticks
in trees.

Polar Bears

Polar bears live on the 'ice-pack'
of the Arctic Ocean.

They are usually solitary animals,
but young bears
stay with their mother
for two or three years.

Polar Bears are about 2.5 m long
They weigh up to 750 kg (males).
The females are smaller

Polar Bears wander huge distances
in search of food.

They eat some fish,
but their chief food is seals.

In summer they eat
great quantities of berries.

More about Polar Bears

Polar Bears are powerful,
inquisitive and active animals.

Eskimos hunt them
for their fur and fat.

Polar Bear flesh
(especially the liver)
is poisonous unless it is
very thoroughly cooked.

In winter Polar Bears do not sleep
as most other bears do,
but the female digs a den
in a deep snowdrift.

Here twin cubs are born.

They are blind for four weeks
and weigh 680 gm.

*A Polar Bear can swim at about 4 kph
and dive to a depth of 15 m.
It can gallop at 40 kph and
jump a 1.8 m snowdrift*

Asiatic Black Bear or Moon Bear

Up to 1.6 m long

This bear is found in Persia,
all through the Himalayas and China
and east to Japan and Formosa.

It lives in leafy forests,
sometimes high up in mountains.

Chinese people like to eat
the paws of these bears.

The Asiatic Black Bear
This is a very aggressive
animal. It sleeps in
winter in a hollow
tree and in
summer in a
tree nest made
of leaves
and twigs

Bears are one of the few animals
which get cavities in their teeth.

This is because, like this bear,
they love sweet food,
such as honey.

Sun Bear

About 1.2 m long.
Found in Burma,
Malaya, Borneo,
Sumatra, Assam
and Indo-China

Most bears live
in cool climates,
but the Sun Bear lives
in hot tropical forests.

This is the smallest bear.

It has quite smooth fur.

It is particularly intelligent.

Sun Bears are expert climbers.
They spend much of their lives
in the tops of tall trees.
Here they search for fruit,
eggs, lizards and birds,
but their favourite food
is honey.

*Sun Bears are active
at night* (nocturnal).
*They do not have a
winter sleep*

27

Sloth Bear

Up to 1.8 m long.
It lives in forests in India and Ceylon

This is one of the strangest
of all bears.

It feeds largely on bees
and termites (white ants),
after breaking up their nests
with its huge curved claws.

The insects are sucked up
through the bear's
specially adapted mouth.

This is a very noisy business.

The cubs of the Sloth
Bear often ride on
the mother's back

Pandas

There are only two species
of Pandas in the world.

The Giant Panda lives
in Chinese mountain forests,
and the Lesser Panda inhabits
mountains of India and China.

Giant Panda

*Lesser
or Red
Panda*

Zoologists usually put Pandas
in the same family *(Procyonidae)*
as the Raccoons,
but there are great differences
between Pandas and Raccoons.

Pandas come from Asia.

Raccoons come from America.

Giant Panda

Up to 1.6 m long and weighing up to 180 kg

The first European
to discover the Giant Panda
was a French missionary
and naturalist called Père David.

This happened in 1869.

We still know very little
about Giant Pandas.

Even today, few people have seen
a wild Giant Panda.

This is because this rare animal
lives in mountain forests
in remote parts of China.

The local people protect it.

The Panda's food

Giant Pandas sometimes eat
fish, birds or small mammals,
but their most usual food
is the shoots and roots of bamboo.

They feed for about ten hours
every day.

The front paws
of Giant Pandas
are adapted so that
they can grasp bamboo shoots.

They feed in a sitting position.

More about
Giant Pandas

Giant Pandas will climb trees,
but usually live on the ground.

In very cold weather
they shelter in caves
or in hollow trees.

Giant Pandas have one or two
very small cubs, which
weigh about 100 g.

Except when they have cubs
Giant Pandas live alone.

Lesser or Red Panda
60 cm long, plus a tail of 40 cm

This beautiful little animal
lives high (up to 3600 m)
in the Himalayas.

It is also found in Western China.

It feeds almost entirely
on plants and fruit,
but may sometimes eat
birds' eggs.

Lesser Pandas live
in family groups.

They move about in single file,
chiefly at night.

By day they sleep in trees.

Some have been kept as pets
in spite of their sharp claws.

The Raccoon family

The Raccoon family is known
as the *Procyonidae*.

It consists of
about sixteen species.

All of them come
from either North or South America.

Common Raccoon
There are seven
different kinds

*Cacomistle
or Ring-tailed 'Cat',
sometimes kept instead
of a cat to keep down mice*

Most members of this family
are quite small.

Most of them are active
in the evening or at night.

All of them have
five toes on each foot.

Common Raccoon

*50 cm long, plus a
tail of 30 cm*

These tough, hardy animals
are found in Canada,
the U S A and as far south
as Central America.

They are experts at surviving,
even in populated places.

They like to live near water
and are good swimmers.

Raccoon's footprints

Right forefoot

Right hindfoot

Raccoons eat frogs, fish,
small animals, fruit and nuts.

In captivity they wash their
food before eating it.

The paws of Raccoons
are rather like human hands
and feet.

More about Raccoons

Raccoons usually have
three or four babies.

These stay with their mother
until they are a year old.

Then they go off to live alone.

*Raccoon washing its food.
They can use their
hands almost as
well as a
monkey can*

Raccoons in northern areas
sleep for most of the winter.

They prepare for this by
eating more to get fat.

All animals which sleep
or hibernate in winter
have to do this to survive.

*The Raccoons' den is
usually in a hollow
tree or rock crevice*

The Kinkajou

*57 cm long, plus
a tail of 45 cm*

*Kinkajous eat
fruit, but are also
very fond of honey*

This is another member
of the Raccoon family.

It lives in the tropical forests
of South and Central America.

It has a *prehensile* tail.

This means that
it can use its tail to grip with.

*There are
three kinds of
Olingo. All live
in Central or
South America*

The Olingo

*40 cm long, plus
a tail of 45 cm*

Olingos are rather like Kinkajous
to look at.

They often mingle with Kinkajous
in the trees,
but their tails are not *prehensile*
and they are thinner
and more 'foxy-faced'.

The Cacomistle or Ring-tailed 'Cat'

35 cm long, plus a tail of 35 cm

This pretty animal lives
in woodland or among rocks.

It comes from the southern parts
of North America, from Oregon
to Mexico.

It is more carnivorous
than most Raccoons,
living mostly on insects.

Although they are shy and nocturnal,
Cacomistles are sometimes kept
as pets.

Three or four young are born
in May or June.

They live for about ten years.

*In South America there
is another kind
of Cacomistle.
It is larger and is silvery grey
in colour*

Coatis

60 cm long, plus a tail of 60 cm

Coatis travel about
in bands made up
of females and young.

These bands can number
from five to a hundred.

Males live alone.

They are known as Coatimundis.

Ring-tailed Coati from South America

Coatis can climb, fight
and swim well.

They will eat anything
they find.

A Coati's nose is used almost
like an elephant's trunk.

It can be turned about
in any direction.

*White-nosed
Coati from
North America*

Index